Stories from the Back Garden

Kathleen Davies

Rock's Mills Press
Oakville, Ontario

There was a little chipmunk
And Chippy was his name.
He lived beneath Kate's house,
His back door near the drain.

Life would have been quite pleasant
If it wasn't for that cat.
Miss Mew kept watch for Chippy
And would have liked him for a snack.
But Kate fed Miss Mew,
She fed her very well.
Chippy was her buddy,
She liked to watch him play.
It made her very happy
When Chippy came to stay.

Little Chippy Chipmunk could not make up his
 mind.
Would he have some sunflower seeds
Or nuts of a certain kind?
Miss Mew the pretty kitty was stretching in the sun.
To chase a little chipmunk would certainly be fun!
But Cheeky Charlie came along and thought that it
 would be
A great game to tease Miss Mew and scold her from
 a tree.

The squirrels were all busy too.
Cheeky Charlie teased Miss Mew.
He'd sit and wait till she was close
Then off he'd go
With Miss Mew in tow!
He'd sit and scold her from a tree
Until there was some other distraction
That sent Miss Mew on another action.

Henrietta Red Squirrel wasn't so bold.
She thought she'd like to live till she got quite old.
She minded her own business and did what she must do.
And while she got her work done
Cheeky Charlie teased Miss Mew.

Henrietta Red Squirrel
Sat in the tree.
She watched Chippy and Miss Mew
Then said "Oh no!
If Kate lets Miss Mew out of her sight
Silly little Chippy will be in an awful plight."

Miss Mew sat in the window

And she would wash and preen

Until she spied Chippy

And then she got quite mean.

She made little growls and twitched her tail

And wasn't a nice cat.

And Kate would say, "Too bad, Miss Mew.

I will not let you out.

This is Chippy's garden too.

He's got a right to play about."

Kate kept Miss Mew in the
    house.
Miss Mew was not very
    pleased.
Chippy peeked in all the
    windows.
I'm afraid he really teased.

Chippy had made Miss Mew very cross.
She sat in the window and glared.
Chippy sat on a rock taunting her.
He didn't care how hard she stared.

Chippy's favourite place to hide
Was beneath the hosta plant.
He'd spy on Miss Mew as she played
And think "What a silly cat!
I'm much too smart for her to catch.
And that is simply that."

Chippy got a bit too smug.
Miss Mew had been
    sleeping on the rug.
He foraged in the
    flowerbed for a
    seed or two.
Miss Mew
    suddenly
    grabbed him.
He thought he'd
    be in a stew.

Miss Mew took Chippy
    right to Kate.
He was all dazed and wet.
Kate grabbed him from Miss Mew.
Should she take him to a vet?

But Chippy got his second wind
And to his hole he ran.
No use to scold Miss Mew
'Cause that is what cats do.
She didn't understand why Kate
wasn't pleased too.
Kate worried all the night.
Was little Chippy all right?
Next morning out of his hole he came.
Chippy was as right as rain.

Now in the barn lived Rackitty Coon.

He liked to sleep when it was light

And then he would come out at night.

While Kate slept

And Miss Mew too,

Rackitty would explore.

He liked to check out the garbage can

That stood near the back door.

Kate would barricade the can.

She'd put a brick on top.

She tried to think of different ways to

make that Rackitty stop.

But Rackitty had many tricks.
He even poked the lid with sticks.
And in the night there'd be a clatter
And the garbage would all scatter.

Chippy would get up at dawn.

He'd sit on a tree trunk and think with a yawn

What messy animals raccoons were.

Chipmunks, on the other hand,

Kept their houses neat and grand.

Under the shed lived Rosy the skunk.

At dusk she came out in search of her supper.

The other animals, though quite proper,

Kept a safe distance from Rosy.

They just didn't get too cosy

Because if she gets cross

She shows them she's the boss

By spraying them with perfume.

And if it's too close

It doesn't smell like a rose.

Better to say "Good evening"

From a safe distance before leaving.

Kate gave Chippy sunflower seeds.
He liked them very well.
He'd fill his little pouches up
Then to his pantry go
And store away the sunflower seeds
For lunch beneath the snow.

Autumn came to Caledon.
The animals were busy.
Chippy and the squirrels
    worked the whole day
    long.
They gathered nuts and
    seeds to keep them
    well and strong.

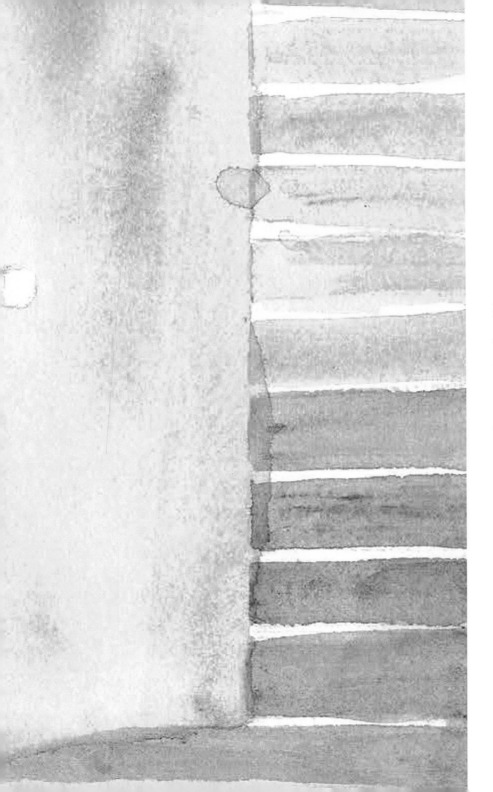

Fall had come upon the land.
Chippy Chipmunk took a stand.
"I have many things to do,
I'll just have to avoid Miss Mew."
There were seeds and nuts to store.
He would just have to watch the back door.

One October day Kate looked for Chippy.
The day became quite crisp and nippy.
Kate, alarmed, began to shout,
"Chippy, where are you?
Please come out!"
Now Chippy had his winter stores
And had just dozed off with little snores
When he heard Kate's frightened shout.
Kate was his friend so he staggered out.
He was a bit dazed and blinked at her.
Kate, relieved, said, "Chippy, I'm sorry.
Go back to sleep and I won't worry."

A blanket of snow covered the land.
Frost was in the air.
Chippy dozed the winter away
In his snug little lair.
Kate thought that Chippy was most sensible of all
To hibernate in a cosy place
When the season became the fall.

Spring had come again

And Kate was glum.

No Chippy to be found.

She watched his many doorways

But no little head peeped out.

Spring turned into early summer,

Kate waited no more.

Then one June morning who should show up at the door?

"Chippy," she squealed, "where have you been?

Did you sleep late or were you away with your mate?

I'm so glad to see you.

I thought you were gone.

I'm so very happy

I could sing a little song."

And so she did.

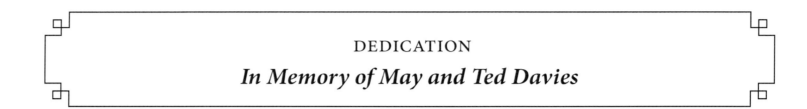

DEDICATION

In Memory of May and Ted Davies

Published by
Rock's Mills Press
www.rocksmillspress.com

The author wishes to express her sincere appreciation to Sarah Carlin-Ball for technical help.

For information about this book, including retail, wholesale and bulk sales arrangements, contact the publisher at customer.service@rocksmillspress.com

Lightning Source UK Ltd.
Milton Keynes UK
UKRC031127201221
395968UK00001B/3

9 781772 442427